This book unfortunately belongs to:

_____

This book is dedicated to cornucopias.

The basket of abundant mystery...

www.ackersbooks.com

Entire World Books: 8

Melanie was too busy shopping for fall boots to help.

ISBN-13: 978-1-951046-14-9

The WORST THANKSGIVING Book

in the Whole Entire World

Joey Acker

Happy Thanksgiving.

But not really.

Because this just so happens to be the worst Thanksgiving book in the whole entire world.

You're probably wondering how a book
about Thanksgiving can be so bad.

Reason #1: I do NOT like Thanksgiving!

You just watch each other eat a bunch of strange, mushy food that you only see once a year and then everyone falls asleep!

THANKSGIVING IS THE BEST!!!

Yep!

Reason #2: Nameful the Rock and a random
chicken are in this book.

What does a chicken have to do with
Thanksgiving?

We're looking for a TURKEY. I'm hungry and it's TURKEY DAY!

Yep!

Well, there are not any turkeys here.

I think you're hiding a TURKEY!

Yep!

What are you talking about?!? I'm trying to tell everyone how much I DON'T like Thanksgiving!

Fine. But I'm watching you!

Yep!

Reason #3: I don't even know what's going on.

GOBBLE!

Oh no...

GOBBLE!

GOBBLE!

Reason #4: I think there really is a turkey
in this book.

Reason #5: I'm the turkey...

But at least you're not a turkey.

That is something to be thankful for.

Hey! I have an idea!

Let's change **THANKSGIVING!**

What kind of food do **YOU** like?

PIZZA OF COURSE!

What is your favorite?

CANDY.

I, Nameless the Rock, do declare that every Thanksgiving shall now be celebrated with pizza and candy.

HELP!!!

Who is this dude?

Reason #6:
Jerry Pumpkins.

You guys have got to help me!

What's wrong,
Jerry?

Reason #7: I'm being chased by a chicken and
a tall rock wearing boots!

They keep yelling,

"PUMPKIN PIE,
PUMPKIN PIE"!

And I think they want to EAT ME!!!

I don't think so!

THE TURKEY IS A

NINJA!

PUMPKIN

PIE!

PUMPKIN

PIE!

HIYAH!

AHHHHHHH!

That was...

AWESOME!!!

I agree!

Now there's just one more
thing we need to do...

HAPPY THANKSGIVING!

Reason #8: The End

Yep!

Made in United States
Orlando, FL
13 November 2022

24510603R00024